Primetime Parable Ministries

PRESENTS

the Mayberry Bible Study

volume 4

study guide

WRITER: **Stephen Skelton**

CREATIVE: **Jim Howell, Judy Northcutt Gaertner**

The Mayberry BIBLE STUDY, *volume 4*
PUBLISHED BY *Primetime Parable Ministries, LLC*

ISBN 0-9765142-5-7

To order or receive more information: *1-877-GOD-IN TV* *(1-877-463-4688)*

INTRODUCTION

Biblical Basis

To illustrate a principle, Jesus often used a parable—an earthly story with a heavenly meaning. Parables allow listeners to recognize real-life events as relevant examples of spiritual truth. In this way, these short stories link what we already know to what we should believe. Those that resist only hear a trivial story, while those that look past the surface find meaning.

Scriptural Precedents

In the parables, Christians have a precedent for utilizing stories for testimony. Interestingly, whether Good Samaritan (Lk 10:30-37), Lost Son (Lk 15:11-32) or Unforgiving Servant (Mt 18:23-35), parable characters did not proclaim the Good News. Indeed, our soap operas today feature similar dramatic narratives. Yet Christ used these secular stories to convey Gospel Truth.

In another direct example, Paul used references from the popular culture to communicate a spiritual message when he quoted certain pagan poets (Ac 17:28) and named the unknown god (Ac 17:22-24). In fact, when Paul said, "'Bad company corrupts good character'" (1 Co 15:33), he was quoting a line of dialogue from a theater play (Greek comedy *Thais* written by Menader).

Modern Parables

Because the Bible is the most influential book in the world, modern writers borrow from it more often than we might think, whether they realize it or not. One fundamental way to use popular entertainment to engage a Christian worldview is to evaluate the story events from a Scriptural perspective. Even a casual conversation about a TV show can afford an opportunity to witness.

To identify God's purposes, first we should examine the overall program in terms of Biblical themes. Next, we should focus that lens on story lines, characters and names. Lastly, we need to use that information as a testimonial tool: mention what a character said about the Lord; uncover the Biblical meaning behind the names; then share how you were saved.

The Mayberry Bible Study

Already, many of you have used this study to successfully reach adults, young people, non-church members—even to refresh the world-weary souls of longtime believers. For those new to the study, ask yourself… Do you want to engage and energize your class… Do you want to bring Jesus to searchers "where they are"… Do you want to model the powerful parable approach of Christ… Then you can use *The Mayberry Bible Study*.

Blessings,

Stephen Skelton
Primetime Parable Ministries

ABOUT THE AUTHOR

Stephen Skelton, founder of Primetime Parable Ministries,
serves as host for *The Mayberry Bible Study*. Previously, he has served
as a writer-producer with Dick Clark Productions and later as head writer for
the television program *America's Dumbest Criminals*. As a Christian in the
entertainment industry, Stephen seeks to identify God's purposes in popular entertainment.
Stephen lives in Nashville, Tennessee with his wife and children.

ABOUT PRIMETIME PARABLE MINISTRIES

At Primetime Parable Ministries, we believe many stories that transcend social,
racial and cultural barriers today do so because they contain spiritual truth
for which all people have a God-given hunger. Accordingly, the ministry promotes
a grassroots approach to using popular entertainment to engage a Christian worldview.
To that end, we hope these Bible studies not only provide a time of good fellowship,
but also continue to equip the church with ways to reach the world beyond.

TABLE OF CONTENTS

THE STORY

This episode, *"Opie and the Spoiled Kid,"* evaluates values when Opie falls under the influence of a spoiled friend! With a sweet bike but a sour attitude, Arnold Winkler convinces Opie that he should do fewer chores for more pay. After Andy Taylor explains his values to Opie, Opie explains his—by holding his breath, crying and pitching a fit! In the end, Andy has to correct Opie—and Arnold—and Mr. Winkler as well! And everyone learns the value of good values!

THE MORAL OF THE STORY

*This lesson, **"The Value of Good Values,"** highlights the Biblical principle of Values. The notes demonstrate that what the world values is temporary—often even here on Earth—but what God values will prove eternal. The study also addresses how God satisfies the righteous but gives craving to the wicked. The goal here is to show how values that are simply allowed to form will follow the world—which is why we should pray for God to help us shape good values.*

the *Mayberry* Bible Study

volume 4• lesson 1

EPISODE TITLE: **"Opie and the Spoiled Kid"**

LESSON TITLE: **"The Value of Good Values"**

BIBLICAL THEME: **Values**

LESSON ONE
"The Value of Good Values"

Unit Overview

Parable

The Moral of Mayberry…

LUKE 16:15

"…What is highly valued among men is detestable in God's sight." (NIV)

Reflection

At the Fishing Hole…

LUKE 12:15

Then he said to them, "Watch out! Be on your guard against all kinds of greed; a man's life does not consist in the abundance of his possessions." (NIV)

Action

Get Out Your Bullet…

PSALM 119:36

Turn my heart toward your statutes and not toward selfish gain. (NIV)

Values

LUKE 16:15

"…What is highly valued among men is detestable in God's sight." (NIV)

It's obvious what we should value, right? Wrong. While the world sees value in wealth, possessions and status, by contrast, God sees value in generosity, kindness and humility. In other words, the world tells us to be selfish, while God tell us to be selfless. So how can we tell which one we are listening to? Check your actions. What things do you think about most? What do you spend the most time doing? Do you find it difficult or easy to be generous, kind or humble? Remember, what the world values is temporary—often even here on Earth—but what God values will prove eternal.

Parable

The Moral of Mayberry…

Here, Opie had his values challenged—and changed for the worse before they got better. Pulled in opposite directions, Opie traveled through a valley between values. On one side, Arnold, not content to be the only rotten one, tried to ruin Opie as well. And on the other side, Andy found himself defending his family values to one of his own family. But Mr. Winkler got the biggest shock when his son valued a bike above all else. Briefly tell how each acted out their values.

Opie: _____

Andy: _____

Arnold: _____

Mr. Winkler: _____

What do you value? How did you develop your values?

_____

_____

_____

_____

Our values reveal us—whether righteous or wicked. Of course, we can see this in others most obviously by their actions. But God can see this spiritually in all men by the state of our souls. **To the soul of the righteous, God provides fulfillment; to the soul of the wicked, God gives nothing but craving—until they find him (Pr 10:3).** *Consider how Arnold acted and why.*

What did Arnold value?
How did Arnold show what he valued?

_____

_____

_____

Was Arnold happy with what he valued?
Did having what he valued satisfy Arnold?

_____

_____

_____

Our vision determines our values. If we focus our vision on worldly goals, our values will arrange themselves to support those pursuits. By contrast, if we focus our vision on Godly goals, we will come to value the long-term rewards of a Godly life. **Much like Moses, our faith in God can enable us to arrange our values around him (Heb 11:26).** Think about what happened to Opie.

What did Opie value? How did Arnold change Opie's values? Why was Arnold able to?

_____

_____

_____

_____

Often, we need someone to help us shape our values. Values that are simply allowed to form usually follow the pattern of the world's values. **As mature Christians, we should first acknowledge we need the power of Christ to combine our faith with our actions (Heb 4:2).** Then our actions will reflect his values, and those values will be worthy of instilling in others.

What did Andy value? How did he try to help Opie to form good values?

_____

_____

_____

_____

Hebrews 11:26
He [Moses] regarded disgrace for the sake of Christ as of greater value than the treasures of Egypt, because he was looking ahead to his reward.

Hebrews 4:2
For we also have had the gospel preached to us, just as they did; but the message they heard was of no value to them, because those who heard did not combine it with faith.

Reflection

At the Fishing Hole...

LUKE 12:15

Then he said to them, "Watch out! Be on your guard against all kinds of greed; a man's life does not consist in the abundance of his possessions." (NIV)

*We must guard our values. If we don't, society—with its emphasis on material possessions—may shape our values for us. Those values are directed toward an earthly kingdom, but Jesus challenges us to direct our values toward the kingdom of heaven. **Placing too much value on the things that make you comfortable in this life reveals a tragic short-sightedness—as well as a lack of faith that God can provide for you (Lk 12:29, 31).** Rather, you should learn to value the things that will make you comfortable for eternity. **In doing so, you will find yourself willing to give up all of the things of earthly value for the kingdom that is of heavenly value (Mt 13:45-46).***

Like Arnold, have your values gotten you into trouble? Give an example.

_____

_____

_____

_____

Luke 12:29, 31

"And do not set your heart on what you will eat or drink; do not worry about it. ... 31) But seek his kingdom, and these things will be given to you as well."

Matthew 13:45-46

"Again, the kingdom of heaven is like a merchant looking for fine pearls. 46) When he found one of great value, he went away and sold everything he had and bought it."

*Mr. Winkler paid the price for bad values. Unfortunately, in our materialistic world, it is difficult not to admire nice possessions, like Arnold's bike. **By the same token, it is all too easy to promote a focus on obtaining earthly treasures—even by questionable methods. However, people that search for happiness in possessions find only recurring dissatisfaction and eventually spiritual death (Pr 10:2).***

Like Mr. Winkler, have you accidentally influenced the wrong values in another? Give an example.

_____

_____

_____

Like Mr. Winkler, have you made an effort
to correct another's values? Give an example.

_____

_____

_____

*Opie had to evaluate his values—the good, the bad and the lazy. Dubious offers such as "less work for more pay" might challenge the values of anyone with an honest work ethic. **Yet whenever you value selfish indulgence over diligent effort, you waste the time you could be proving useful both to yourself and others. Show that you value the time God has given you (Pr 10:4-5).***

Like Opie, have you had your values challenged—
either for worse or for better? Give an example.

_____

_____

_____

> Proverbs 10:2
> Ill-gotten treasures are of no value, but righteousness delivers from death.

> Proverbs 10:4-5
> Lazy hands make a man poor, but diligent hands bring wealth.
> 5) He who gathers crops in summer is a wise son, but he who sleeps during harvest is a disgraceful son.

Action

Get Out Your Bullet...

> **PSALM 119:36**
> *Turn my heart toward your statutes and not toward selfish gain.* (NIV)

Luke 12:33-34
"Sell your possessions and give to the poor. Provide purses for yourselves that will not wear out, a treasure in heaven that will not be exhausted...34) For where your treasure is, there your heart will be also."

Romans 2:7-8
Those who by persistence in doing good seek glory, honor and immortality, he will give eternal life. 8) But for those who are self-seeking and who reject the truth and follow evil, there will be wrath and anger.

You should pray for God to shape your values. This is the most important action you can take to control yourself. Apart from God, you will surely value material things as a means to selfish security. But true success has less to do with a little money than an entire kingdom—the kingdom of heaven. Being a citizen of this kingdom means making Christ the King of your life. **When you do this, his selfless values will begin to become your own (Lk 12:33-34).** *Then your faith will free you from the anxiety that always follows a focus on money.* **On the day you stand before the King, you will be focused on either leaving behind your earthly treasures or receiving your heavenly reward (Ro 2:7).** *Value the latter.*

Why should you develop good values?

_____

_____

_____

_____

How can you develop good values?

_____

_____

_____

_____

_____

What do "good values" hold important?

_____

_____

_____

_____

_____

What values have your actions revealed lately?

How can you show better values?

_____

_____

_____

_____

_____

THE STORY

This episode, **"Aunt Bee's Medicine Man,"** flirts with temptation
when a medicine man lures Aunt Bee with a cure that is really
bad medicine! When Aunt Bee worries over her age, she becomes
vulnerable to the conman Colonel Harvey. After he offers an elixir to
fix her, Aunt Bee eagerly gives in. Only later does Andy discover the
cure-all is almost all-alcohol! And a sober Aunt Bee realizes that this
medicine man had no remedy, only a prescription for temptation.

THE MORAL OF THE STORY

*This lesson, **"A Prescription for Temptation,"** highlights
the Biblical principle of Temptation. The study examines how
spiritually empty people are tempted much more easily than
those filled with spiritual security. The lesson also addresses how
we should work to recognize what tempts us, turn from that
temptation and continually pray that we are not drawn back
into it. The point of this study is that the only way we can resist
temptation is to know, believe and obey God's Word.*

the Mayberry Bible Study

volume 4 • lesson 2

EPISODE TITLE: **"Aunt Bee's Medicine Man"**

LESSON TITLE: **"A Prescription for Temptation"**

BIBLICAL THEME: **Temptation**

LESSON TWO
"A Prescription for Temptation"

<u>Unit Overview</u>
Parable
The Moral of Mayberry…

> MATTHEW 26:41
> *"Watch and pray so that you will not fall into temptation. The spirit is willing, but the body is weak."* (NIV)

Reflection
At the Fishing Hole…

> 1 CORINTHIANS 10:13
> *No temptation has seized you except what is common to man. And God is faithful; he will not let you be tempted beyond what you can bear. But when you are tempted, he will also provide a way out so that you can stand up under it.* (NIV)

Action
Get Out Your Bullet…

> JAMES 1:13-14
> *When temped, no one should say, "God is tempting me." For God cannot be tempted by evil, nor does he tempt anyone; but each one is tempted when, by his own evil desire, he is dragged away and enticed.* (NIV)

Temptation

MATTHEW 26:41

"Watch and pray so that you will not fall into temptation. The spirit is willing, but the body is weak." (NIV)

It seems some of us watch out for temptations so we can be sure to take full advantage of them. Instead, Jesus warns Peter to watch and pray so that he will not give in to temptations. Prayer is important because it focuses us on God, from whom we derive our strength to resist temptation. When we focus more on the object of our temptation than God, that thing becomes a false god, from which we cannot draw any strength. In this way, through the areas we choose to be weak in, we give our temptations power over us.

Parable

The Moral of Mayberry...

When Aunt Bee convinced herself she was weak, she made the Colonel's allure of a cure seem stronger. Driven by doubts she allowed to creep in, she set up herself to be enticed. Meanwhile, the Colonel was too busy counting his cash to count the cost of his temptations. Luckily, Andy spared himself by focusing on feeling fine—then he spared others by telling what a tempter the Colonel really was. Briefly describe how each interacted with temptation.

Aunt Bee: _____

Andy: _____

Colonel Harvey: _____

Ladies Aid: _____

What tempts you? How do you resist temptation?

_____

_____

_____

> **Matthew 4:3-4**
> The tempter came to him and said, "If you are the Son of God, tell these stones to become bread." 4| Jesus answered, "It is written: 'Man does not live on bread alone, but on every word that comes from the mouth of God.' "

We are often tempted at our weakest point. One reason this happens is because Satan watches for a time to attack. **When Christ was tempted in the wilderness, he used Scripture to repel Satan (Mt 4:3-4).** *So can we. The weaker we feel in an area, the stronger our knowledge should be on what the Bible says about that area. Consider how Colonel Harvey "attacked" Aunt Bee.*

How did Colonel Harvey tempt Aunt Bee?
How did he play upon her weaknesses?

_____

_____

_____

> **Matthew 4:9-10**
> "All this I will give you," he said, "if you will bow down and worship me." 10| Jesus said to him, "Away from me, Satan! For it is written: 'Worship the Lord your God, and serve him only.' "

Sometimes we set up ourselves to be tempted. We do this when we put ourselves into a position that places us at a disadvantage. **To be strong, we should focus on God and serve him only (Mt 4:9-10).** *Spiritually lost people are tempted much more easily than those with spiritual security. Think about how Aunt Bee allowed herself to be tempted—and how Andy did not.*

How did Aunt Bee set up herself to be tempted?
What made her vulnerable?

_____

_____

_____

_____

Why wasn't Andy tempted? How did he resist the Colonel's temptation?

_____

_____

_____

_____

*Those that have given into temptation must be dealt with swiftly—and gently. We should reach out with reconciliation, rather than strike them with condemnation. **At the same time, our correction should not be without backbone, lest in comforting the tempted we should fall prey to the same temptation (Gal 6:1).** Act in humility to both the sinner and the Lord of you and them.*

> Galatians 6:1
> Brothers, if someone is caught in a sin, you who are spiritual should restore him gently. But watch yourself, or you also may be tempted.

How did Andy help others face their temptation?
What was important about his method?

_____

_____

_____

_____

Reflection

At the Fishing Hole…

> 1 CORINTHIANS 10:13
> **No temptation has seized you except what is common to man. And God is faithful; he will not let you be tempted beyond what you can bear. But when you are tempted, he will also provide a way out so that you can stand up under it.** *(NIV)*

Matthew 4:1
Then Jesus was led by the Spirit into the desert to be tempted by the devil.

Hebrews 2:18
Because he himself suffered when he was tempted, he is able to help those who are being tempted.

Everyone is tempted. But not everyone gives in. With God's help, anyone can resist any temptation. Often, we get ourselves into trouble by tempting temptation. Instead, we should train ourselves to recognize what tempts us, turn from that temptation and continually pray that we are not drawn back into that trap. **The fact that we are tempted does not make us sinful. Christ demonstrated this when he was tempted by Satan in the desert (Mt 4:1).** *Times of temptation can build character if we do not give in.* **Remember, Christ was tempted—and he will not leave you alone in your temptations (Heb 2:18).**

Like Aunt Bee, have your insecurities made you prone to temptations? Give an example.

_____

_____

Like Andy, have you made an effort to avoid temptations? Give an example.

_____

_____

_____

_____

As bad as Aunt Bee felt before she gave in to temptation, afterward she felt worse. The shame we often feel after giving in usually outweighs the momentary pleasure the temptation brought. One reason we feel disappointed in ourselves is because we sense that we have failed a test. **Indeed, while God does not lead us into temptation, he does allow us to be tested with the choice to sin or be delivered (Mt 6:13).**

> Matthew 6:13
> And lead us not into temptation, but deliver us from the evil one.

Like Aunt Bee, have you suffered the consequences of giving into temptation? Give an example.

_____

_____

_____

_____

If Andy was tempted to judge Aunt Bee, you would have never known it. Sympathy for others, based on our understanding of our own weaknesses, can lessen the temptation to pass judgment on those that have given in. **Similarly, we are blessed to have a Savior who is able to sympathize and provide an example for not giving into temptation (Heb 4:15).**

> Hebrews 4:15
> For we do not have a high priest who is unable to sympathize with our weaknesses, but we have one who has been tempted in every way, just as we are— yet was without sin.

Unlike Andy, have you judged those who have given in to temptation? Give an example.

_____

_____

_____

Action
Get Out Your Bullet...

JAMES 1:13-14

When temped, no one should say, "God is tempting me." For God cannot be tempted by evil, nor does he tempt anyone; but each one is tempted when, by his own evil desire, he is dragged away and enticed.   (NIV)

Psalm 103:5
who satisfies your desires with good things so that your youth is renewed like the eagle's.

Luke 4:1-2
Jesus, full of the Holy Spirit, returned from the Jordan and was led by the Spirit into the desert, 2/ where for forty days he was tempted by the devil. He ate nothing during those days, and at the end of them he was hungry.

Sometimes when a temptation overpowers us, our very next temptation is to blame God. However, in using this excuse or any other, we refuse to accept responsibility for our own actions. Instead, we should acknowledge our sin, so that we can confess and receive forgiveness. **Only when we recognize our own weaknesses can we begin to understand how God can satisfy our desires (Ps 103:5). Conversely, temptation can also come through our areas of strength, after an accomplishment or triumph, as it did with Christ (Lk 4:1-2).** *In either event, the only way that we can consistently resist temptation is through knowing, believing and obeying God's Word.*

Why should you resist temptation?

_____

_____

_____

What could you do to avoid temptation?

_____

_____

_____

_____

Why does God allow us to be tempted?

_____

_____

_____

_____

How will you deal with the next temptation?
How can you help others to resist?

_____

_____

_____

_____

THE STORY

This episode, **"Rafe Hollister Sings,"** croons about encouragement as Andy inspires a farmer to represent Mayberry in the town musicale! Rafe Hollister is the friendly farmer with the voice of an angel—and an earthy look about him that rubs the Mayor wrong. Although Andy tries to dress Rafe up, the Mayor still puts Rafe down. Finally, Andy decides to support Rafe as Rafe and even joins him on stage—all in an effort to offer his farmer friend some sound encouragement!

THE MORAL OF THE STORY

*This lesson, **"Sound Encouragement,"** highlights the Biblical principle of Encouragement. The notes look at how encouragement can play a key role in helping others, as well as ourselves, to maintain faith. This study also explains that because the Christian intention is always to help, any criticism must focus on lifting others out of sin and closer to Christ. The core message here is that Christian encouragement has the power to prevent depression, apathy, even unbelief.*

the *Mayberry* Bible Study

volume 4 • lesson 3

EPISODE TITLE: **"Rafe Hollister Sings"**

LESSON TITLE: **"Sound Encouragement"**

BIBLICAL THEME: **Encouragement**

LESSON THREE
"Sound Encouragement"

<u>Unit Overview</u>

Parable

The Moral of Mayberry...

> HEBREWS 3:13
> *But encourage one another daily, as long as it is called Today,*
> *so that none of you may be hardened by sin's deceitfulness* (NIV)

Reflection

At the Fishing Hole...

> ROMANS 12:6-8
> *We have different gifts, according to the grace given us.*
> *If a man's gift is prophesying, let him use it in proportion to his*
> *faith. If it is serving, let him serve; if it is teaching, let him teach;*
> *if it is encouraging, let him encourage...* (NIV)

Action

Get Out Your Bullet...

> HEBREWS 10:25
> *Let us not give up meeting together, as some are in the*
> *habit of doing, but let us encourage one another—and all the more*
> *as you see the Day approaching.* (NIV)

23

Encouragement

HEBREWS 3:13

But encourage one another daily, as long as it is called Today, so that none of you may be hardened by sin's deceitfulness (NIV)

Why are we so quick to criticize and so slow to encourage? Why do we sometimes feel better when we make another seem worse? Or alternately, why do we find it hard to say something that lifts up someone else—especially, over ourselves? Out of love, there may come a time to point out another's faults. But first, we should take many more opportunities to encourage that person if we are to build his or her trust. If we are truly trying to help others instead of ourselves, we can see clearly that one of the best ways to be a benefit is to offer them encouragement.

Parable

The Moral of Mayberry...

Rafe was encouraged to sing when Andy sang his praises. When it came to their farmer friend, Andy tried to support Rafe as much as Barney tried to undermine him. Tellingly, Andy had nothing to gain by encouraging Rafe, while Barney had a lot to lose by *not* discouraging him. Meanwhile, the Mayor and Mrs. Jeffries snobbishly withheld approval—right up until everyone in the Musicale audience applauded Rafe. Briefly, describe how each dealt with encouragement.

Rafe: _____

Andy: _____

Barney: _____

Mayor: _____

Mrs. Jeffries: _____

Have you been encouraged? Have you encouraged other people?
For both, what happened?

_____

_____

_____

_____

> **Romans 15:5**
> May the God who gives endurance and encouragement give you a spirit of unity among yourselves as you follow Christ Jesus

Encouragement comes from unity. In general, we encourage those toward whom we feel love. Christ loves everyone, and holds encouragement for everyone who loves him. **As Christians, we should have this spirit of unity toward others, treating their problems, as well as their triumphs, as our own (Ro 15:5).** *Consider how Andy acted toward Rafe—and why.*

How did Andy encourage Rafe? Why did he
make the effort to encourage a farmer to sing?

_____

_____

_____

> **1 Thessalonians 5:9, 11**
> For God did not appoint us to suffer wrath but to receive salvation through our Lord Jesus Christ... 11) Therefore encourage one another and build each other up, just as in fact you are doing.

Should Christians criticize? Sometimes we must. However, the Christian intention is always to help people, not hurt them. Therefore, any criticism must be directed toward lifting others out of sin and closer to Christ. **Because of the encouraging promise we have in God, Christians have no other reason to be negative (1 Th 5:9, 11).** *Consider what Andy said to Barney—and what he didn't say.*

Did Andy criticize Barney? Would he have been
correct to do so? For either way, why?

_____

_____

_____

_____

*Watch out for those who would rather divide than
encourage.* **Keep your distance from people that
think only of benefiting themselves, even at the
expense of those around them (Ro 16:17-18).**
*Although some of these people may call themselves
Christians, their self-centered thoughts and unkind words
demonstrate that they are not followers of Christ.*

Romans 16:17-18
I urge you, brothers,
to watch out for those
who cause divisions and
put obstacles in your
way that are contrary
to the teaching you
have learned... 18) For
such people are not
serving our Lord Christ,
but their own appetites.

Why did Barney discourage Rafe?
Why did he try to stop Rafe from trying out?

_____

_____

_____

Why did the Mayor and Mrs. Jeffries withhold support?
What was more important to them?

_____

_____

_____

_____

Reflection

At the Fishing Hole...

ROMANS 12:6-8

We have different gifts, according to the grace given us. If a man's gift is prophesying, let him use it in proportion to his faith. If it is serving, let him serve; if it is teaching, let him teach; if it is encouraging, let him encourage... (NIV)

1 Thessalonians 4:16-18
For the Lord himself will come down from heaven... and the dead in Christ will rise first. 17) After that, we who are still alive and are left will be caught up together with them... 18) Therefore encourage each other with these words.

Encouragement is a gift—to both the giver and the receiver. It is an ability God has especially blessed some with so that they might bless others. However, each and every one of us should be ready with a kind word for another person, no matter the circumstance. **Through fellowship, we can remind each other of the meaning of the Good News, the great reward of resurrection (1 Th 4:16-18).** With love, concern and acceptance our encouragement can play a key role in helping others, as well as ourselves, to maintain faith. **Even the way in which we live can offer inspiration as others see us dealing with difficulties through good deeds and words because of the encouragement of God (2 Th 2:16-17).**

2 Thessalonians 2:16-17
May our Lord Jesus Christ himself and God our Father, who loved us and by his grace gave us eternal encouragement and good hope, 17) encourage your hearts and strengthen you in every good deed and word.

Like Andy, have you encouraged someone in an area that is new to him? Give an example.

_____

_____

_____

_____

Although Rafe had more reasons to become discouraged, he remained encouraged. Likewise, as Christians, when faced with persecution, our faith is tried. During these times, we need endurance alongside encouragement to support us until the trouble has passed. **In a greater sense, for those of us who persevere in doing the will of God, he promises an everlasting reward (Heb 10:36).**

Hebrews 10:36
You need to persevere so that when you have done the will of God, you will receive what he has promised.

Like Rafe, have others discouraged you from accomplishing something? Give an example.

_____

_____

_____

If Andy had discouraged Rafe, he would've joined the majority. We may stand alone in encouraging a friend—and that may be all the more reason to do it! Conversely, consider how much their encouragement would mean to you if the situation was reversed. **Regardless of whether it is fashionable, we should correct those that are wrong and encourage those that are right (2 Ti 4:2).**

2 Timothy 4:2
Preach the Word; be prepared in season and out of season; correct, rebuke, and encourage—with great patience and careful instruction.

Like Andy, have you encouraged someone when others discouraged him? Give an example.

_____

_____

Like Rafe, have you needed encouragement from another to give you hope? Give an example.

_____

_____

_____

Action
Get Out Your Bullet...

HEBREWS 10:25

Let us not give up meeting together, as some are in the habit of doing, but let us encourage one another—and all the more as you see the Day approaching. (NIV)

Philippians 1:14
Because of my chains, most of the brothers in the Lord have been encouraged to speak the word of God more courageously and fearlessly.

Philippians 2:1
If you have any encouragement from being united with Christ, if any comfort from his love, if any fellowship with the Spirit, if any tenderness and compassion, 2) then make my joy complete by being like-minded...

Encouragement happens in community. Only when we are with others do we have an opportunity to both encourage and be encouraged. This encouragement is crucial as we draw closer to Judgment Day.  **As Christians, when we face difficult times, we should encourage one another in our faith (Ph 1:14).** *Your kind words may make the difference between someone dropping out or coming through. Often the person that is alone is the one that needs encouragement the most. Encouragement can prevent negative feelings, such as depression, apathy, even unbelief.* **Of course, encouragement with this kind of life-changing power can only flow from Christ (Ph 2:1).**

Why should you encourage others?

_____

_____

_____

_____

When should you criticize someone?

_____

_____

_____

_____

Why do you need encouragement?

_____

_____

_____

_____

Whom should you encourage next?
How will you encourage that person?

_____

_____

_____

_____

THE STORY

This episode, *"The Rivals,"* leads to a story on guidance as Opie seeks a guide and gets three—Andy, Barney and Thelma Lou too! When Opie sets his heart on his little friend Karen, Andy advises him to be as nice as he can to her. Then when Karen seems to ignore Opie, Thelma Lou provides a delicious distraction with fudge brownies. But when Barney gets jealous of Thelma Lou and Opie, the Deputy comes off like a demented mentor—and demonstrates exactly why nice guides finish first!

THE MORAL OF THE STORY

This lesson, "Nice Guides Finish First," highlights the Biblical principle of Guidance. The study concentrates on how we should seek guidance because the perception of one person can be hindered by bias, misunderstanding or lack of knowledge. The notes also point out that, ironically, when we fail to seek the guidance of the Lord, we can actually fail to serve our own best interests. In summary, this lesson shows that, although we often seek guidance out of doubt, confusion or fear, because God is our Savior, his guidance always gives us a reason to be hopeful.

the Mayberry *Bible Study*

volume 4 • lesson 4

EPISODE TITLE: **"The Rivals"**

LESSON TITLE: **"Nice Guides Finish First"**

BIBLICAL THEME: **Guidance**

LESSON FOUR
"Nice Guides Finish First"

Unit Overview

Parable

The Moral of Mayberry...

> PROVERBS 11:14
>
> *For lack of guidance a nation falls, but many advisers make victory sure.* (NIV)

Reflection

At the Fishing Hole...

> PSALM 48:14
>
> *For this God is our God for ever and ever; he will be our guide even to the end.* (NIV)

Action

Get Out Your Bullet...

> PSALM 25:4-5
>
> *Show me your ways, O LORD, teach me your paths;*
> *guide me in your truth and teach me, for you are God my Savior,*
> *and my hope is in you all day long.* (NIV)

Guidance

> **PROVERBS 11:14**
>
> *For lack of guidance a nation falls, but many advisers make victory sure.* (*NIV*)

We all need guidance. Even a great leader needs a greater guide. Only a fool leads himself—and we should pity those that follow him. The perception of one person can be hindered by bias, misunderstanding or lack of knowledge. In fact, seeking guidance from counselors is a mark of wisdom. Are you wise enough to follow the words of those who can lead you in the right way? Ironically, when we fail to seek the guidance of the Lord, we can actually fail to serve our own best interests. Develop the desire to be guided by reading God's guidebook, the Bible.

Parable

The Moral of Mayberry…

When Opie needed a guide, he got three—but only two were worth following. To lead Opie past the first pangs of puppy love, Andy gave guidance worthy of a father, and Thelma Lou gave guidance worthy of a friend. But Barney gave guidance mostly to serve himself, which suitably led him further down the wrong path. In the end, with the right guides, Opie found his way, while once again Barney found himself hopelessly lost. Briefly, describe how each handled guidance.

Opie: _____

Andy _____

Barney: _____

Thelma Lou: _____

Have you followed someone's guidance?

Have you given someone guidance? For both, what happened?

_____

_____

_____

_____

> Psalm 25:9
> He guides the humble in what is right and teaches them his way.

The first step to being guided is to want to be guided. Some of us resist seeking guidance until it is our last resort. Instead, we should seek guidance daily in matters both big and small. **Without a desire for guidance, we are left to lead ourselves, often proudly and in the wrong direction. Conversely, God guides the humble in his way (Ps 25:9).** *Consider why Opie asked for advice.*

Why did Opie seek guidance? How did he show wisdom in asking for guidance?

_____

_____

_____

> Proverbs 4:10-11
> Listen, my son, accept what I say, and the years of your life will be many. 11) I guide you in the way of wisdom and lead you along straight paths.

What makes a good guide "good"? Often, it is the source from which he draws his counsel. If that source is his own life, look at how he has lived. Determine whether or not he has applied wise principles to himself. **We should eagerly seek guidance from those who demonstrate they have walked with wisdom (Pr 4:10-11).** *Think about the qualifications of Andy and Barney as guides.*

What guidance did Andy offer to Opie?

Was this good advice? Why or why not?

_____

_____

_____

_____

Was Barney qualified to give guidance?

How did his lack of compassion hinder him?

_____

_____

_____

_____

*Guides can come in many different forms. Some of them may look like friends instead of mentors. **In seeking guidance on a plan, remain open to multiple counselors, even if at first not all of their ways seem to address the problem directly (Pr 15:22)**. Success with a problem may be achieved by viewing it from different angles—or even not looking at it at all for a moment.*

Proverbs 15:22
Plans fail for lack of counsel, but with many advisers they succeed.

How did Thelma Lou offer guidance?

How helpful was she by simply being there?

_____

_____

_____

_____

Reflection

At the Fishing Hole...

PSALM 48:14

For this God is our God for ever and ever; he will be our guide even to the end. *(NIV)*

Proverbs 16:23
A wise man's heart guides his mouth, and his lips promote instruction.

John 16:13
"But when he, the Spirit of truth, comes, he will guide you into all truth."

*God wants to be our Guide, even to the end—and he knows the way there. This demonstrates three important characteristics of any guide: knowledge, vision and love. **Along with knowing the way, a guide should consider how his counsel will affect you and advise out of genuine care (Pr 16:23).** Without these, both the guide and the seeker are in the dark. God offers guidance with knowledge, vision and love through the Bible. **If we will humbly submit to the Word, the Holy Spirit will guide us in God's truth, the truth of Jesus Christ (Jn 16:13).** Following this way leads to peace. Pridefully going our own way leads to despair—an end no one wants.*

Like Opie, have you showed humility
in asking for guidance?   Give an example.

_____

_____

_____

Like Barney, have you been in need of guidance
but too proud to seek it? Give an example.

_____

_____

_____

In getting guidance, Opie helped Karen as well. When we act on wise counsel, we often benefit more than just ourselves. For this reason, not only should we seek guides but we should urge others to seek them also. **In the absence of guidance, we may become like the blind leading the blind, causing both ourselves and the ones with us to fail (Mt 15:14).**

Like Karen, have you benefited from someone else receiving guidance? Give an example.

_____

_____

_____

_____

If Karen had anyone to offer her guidance, we didn't see them. Some people may find themselves in a similar situation without an obvious guide or mentor from whom they can seek advice. However, even when a human counselor is not available, our heavenly counselor always is. **Just as sheep look to their shepherd, so we can look to the Lord and he will guide us (Ps 23:1-3).**

Like Karen, have you been in need of guidance with no one to offer it? Give an example.

_____

_____

_____

Matthew 15:14
"Leave them; they are blind guides. If a blind man leads a blind man, both will fall into a pit."

Psalm 23:1-3
The LORD is my shepherd, I shall not be in want. 2) He makes me lie down in green pastures, he leads me beside quiet waters, 3) he restores my soul. He guides me in paths of righteousness for his name's sake.

Action

Get Out Your Bullet...

PSALM 25:4-5

Show me your ways, O Lord, teach me your paths; guide me in your truth and teach me, for you are God my Savior, and my hope is in you all day long. (NIV)

> John 10:11
>
> "I am the good shepherd. The good shepherd lays down his life for the sheep."

> John 14:26
>
> "But the Counselor, the Holy Spirit, whom the Father will send in my name, will teach you all things and will remind you of everything I have said to you."

God guides us in truth, which gives us hope. Often we seek guidance out of doubt, confusion or fear. Sometimes the human guidance we receive does nothing to ease those worries. Yet, because he is our Savior, the guidance of God always gives us a reason to be optimistic. When seeking guidance, our impatience with uncertainty can cause us to demand immediate answers. **Instead, as the good shepherd, Christ offers to lead us in his way (Jn 10:11).** *Indeed, without having walked with Jesus, answers alone would provide merely temporary relief.* **Only by being guided by the Holy Spirit can we grow to be more like Christ (Jn 14:26).** *And only when we are more like Christ should we offer guidance to others.*

Why should you seek guidance?

_____

_____

_____

_____

From whom should you seek guidance?

_____

_____

_____

_____

When are you ready to give guidance?

_____

_____

_____

_____

What is the next issue you will need guidance in?

When will you seek that guidance?

_____

_____

_____

_____

_____

From your friends at

Primetime Parable Ministries

Want to know what's next?

Want to hear when it's out?

Other questions or comments?

Then call us at
1-877-GOD-IN TV
(1-877-463-4688).

We look forward to serving you!

Blessings,

Stephen Skelton

Stephen Skelton
Primetime Parable Ministries

DEDICATION:
*Father
Son
Holy Spirit*